American edition published in 2020
by New Frontier Publishing USA,
an imprint of New Frontier Publishing Europe Ltd
www.newfrontierpublishing.us

First published in the UK in 2019
by New Frontier Publishing Europe Ltd
Uncommon, 126 New King's Road, London, SW6 4LZ
www.newfrontierpublishing.co.uk

ISBN: 978-1-912858-81-1

Distributed in the United States and Canada by Lerner Publishing Group Inc
241 First Avenue North, Minneapolis, MN 55401 USA
www.lernerbooks.com

Library of Congress Cataloging-in-Publication Data is available.

Designed by Verity Clark

Printed in China
10 9 8 7 6 5 4 3 2 1

Under the Same Sky

For Alexia and Jerome:
live with others in mind
~ R V

For my dear friend Jo,
from across the miles
~ N J

Under the Same Sky

Robert Vescio   Nicky Johnston

NEW FRONTIER PUBLISHING

I know you're out there.
I can't see you but I know you're there.

I call out to you to say hello.

But the distance between us
makes it hard to reach.

We are like the sun and the moon … always seeking.

Always missing each other.

We are like the sky and the sea ...

… always apart. Never touching.

Longing to be friends ...

... but wondering if it can ever be.

I rest with the stars

as you rise with the sun.

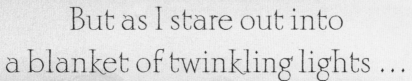

But as I stare out into
a blanket of twinkling lights …

My mind races.

My heart thumps.

Sometimes things

have a way

of just coming together.

from up high,

from in between,

or from up close.

An unexpected surprise
can make a difference.

It can brighten a dark sky

and make the dark not feel so dark.

It can make a heart beat a little faster ...

...and bring us close.